CROSSWAY BOOKS . WHEATON, ILLINOIS
A DIVISION OF GOOD NEWS PUBLISHERS

A Treasure Beyond Measure

Design by Cindy Kiple

Published by Crossway Books
a division of Good News Publishers
1300 Crescent Street
Wheaton, Illinois 60187

First printing, 2001

Printed in Canada

ISBN 1-58134-343-4

10 09 08 07 06 05 04 03 02 01
15 14 13 12 11 10 9 8 7 6 5 4 3 2 1

To Joe and Joyce Brown and Family
Thanks for the treasured childhood memories
of "hanging out" at your place!

Love and Appreciation,
Melody

For the Henderson Family

Steve

THE LOST LAMB
4 SPEED
FARMER BROWN'S FIELD TRIP
IT ISN'T FUNNY, I'VE LOST MY MONEY
THE OTHER BROTHER
GRACIE'S WORLD

Now Fred was a guy like you or me,
He lived in a house and watched TV.
One day he thought: *There must be more—*
This life of mine is just a bore!

So Fred went out for a walk that day
And found a shop along his way.
He saw some books and a red stuffed fox,
One brass lantern, and an old carved box.

Nathan
TYLER
MDB
KDB
SF

Inside that box in a silken wrap,
Was an ancient hidden treasure map.
Fred thought this map looked pretty nice,
And figured it was worth its price.

N
POLE VAULTING
MICHAEL DODGE
treasure

The map was marked, now quite specific,
To an island in the South Pacific.
He used a rule so he could measure
Exactly where to find his treasure.

Fred sold his house and quit his job.
He bought a boat and a good hound-dog.
He spent his cash for food and stuff,
Then filled his boat—more than enough!

So off Fred sailed one sunny day,
Beneath the bridge and past the bay.
At last, at last! Adventure-bound
With his map and boat and fine new hound!

But halfway there, a storm brewed up.
The boat was lost, but not the pup.
Fred saved his box and saved his dog.
They rode the waves on a floating log.

It took all day ’til they reached land
And flopped, exhausted, on the sand.
Fred placed his box upon his lap.
It held his watch and treasure map.

Fred studied the map by setting sun.
This isle was surely not the one.
Without money and without food,
He told his dog, “This don’t look good.”

N

TIKI-LAND CAFE

So Fred got a job washing dishes,
Scrubbing pots, and cleaning fishes.
He worked real hard and saved each cent.
They slept on the beach to save on rent.

TIKI-LAND CAFE

Fred worked and saved and bought a boat.
It looked a wreck, but it could float.
He loaded it up with stuff he scrounged,
Then climbed aboard with his fine hound.

It took eight days and seven nights
Until his island came in sight!
Fred docked the boat right on the sand,
And off he jumped onto dry land.

By now Fred knew his map by heart.
He knew the spot. He had to start.
"Not so fast!" said a wee little man.
"Don't you know I own this land?"

"I don't have much—my name is Fred.
I'll trade my boat and watch," he said.
"All I need is a speck of land."
The stranger grinned and shook his hand.

Fred dug all day and all night too.
It must be here—it must, he knew.
At dawn's first light, he heard the clank—
And down upon his knees he sank!

"This is it!" he told his hound.
And the two of them just danced around.
Now Fred is wealthy beyond measure,
All because he sought his treasure.

Again, the kingdom of heaven is

like treasure hidden in a field,

which a man found and hid;

and for joy over it he goes

and sells all that he has

and buys that field.

MATTHEW 13:44
(NKJV)